World Wrestling

Series 1: Birth Of Legends

Book 1

Night Of Warriors

By El Haggisso

Do not try the wrestling moves in this book at home. They are dangerous and some of them the famous wrestling stars of today could not even do safely.

Some moves could be practiced on your pillow or your sister's teddy, but some are even too dangerous for that.

You can try these moves out with your action figures. However, it may cause damage to your figure or your pillow and sister's teddy for that matter. So be careful.

This book is for El Sueño y El Lobo Verde

ISBN: 9781977014665

Author's Note

I am El Haggisso, a semi-retired masked wrestler. I wrestled in the W.W.W federation for almost all of my career. WWW stands for World Wrestling Warriors and it is the world renowned company owned and managed by the famous promoter Big Ernie Dallas. Now that I am semi-retired (which means I no longer wrestle regularly, but do fight on special occasions), I have decided to write my story. I was going to write a traditional autobiography, but I realised that people would be interested in all the wonderful and terrible wrestlers in the W.W.W glory years and not just me. People may know the history told by the W.W.W, but they do not know what really happened. They don't know what happened behind the scenes. I am one of a handful of people who can tell this tale as an insider who has been with the company since it began.

This book deals with the very beginning of the W.W.W, when Big Ernie invited the world's most famous wrestlers to join the first global wrestling company. At this time I was not El Haggisso. I was a ten year old Scottish boy living with his dad in a caravan.

El Haggisso

Chapter 1: The Invitation

My name was Jock Baxter and I was a 10 year old boy who lived in a caravan with his dad. My dad was called Davie Baxter. He was a Scottish wrestler who wrestled for various British wrestling promotions with his tag team partner and fellow Scot, Mark Stuart. They were called The Bax-Stu Boys, which in fairness was a terrible name. But they were popular wherever they wrestled and had been Scottish Tag Team Champions 4 times in the Scottish Gladiators Wrestling federation and UK Tag Team Champions twice.

We lived in a small white caravan together, that my dad pulled around the country in his old car. He didn't make a lot of money wrestling in the UK, but it was the thing he loved to do. Other wrestlers stayed in hotels when they wrestled in different towns and cities, but dad wanted a more stable upbringing for me so we took our caravan. Luckily most of his wrestling events were at the weekend so we spent most of the time in Edinburgh where I went to school. We still stayed in the caravan though, it was our only home. If dad did have to work away in the week, I went to my gran's house. I enjoyed school and loved to be with my gran, but I always looked forward to the weekend. To the wrestling.

The real adventure began one night when we had just settled into the caravan after my dad had wrestled a match in Liverpool. The Bax-Stu Boys had beaten a tough local team called The Liver Lads in a great match. Dad was sitting watching the tv and munching a kebab we had picked up on the way home. My dad, Davie Baxter, was a fantastic wrestler. He was strong, quick, athletic, had great technique and he had excellent stamina. His only problem was that he was quite short. He was only 5 foot 9 and most other successful wrestlers were a lot taller. But to me he was the greatest wrestler in the world. He was my hero.

He ran a hand through his long brown hair as he ate, spilling a bit of sauce on his hairy chest. He was a bit scruffy, not wearing a shirt as he sat in dirty old jeans. Gran said that's why mum had left him for a wrestler from London called Mr Smooth. We both hated Mr Smooth! And to be honest, which I suppose I have to be if this is going to be a true story, we both hated mum.

A loud knock at the door interrupted our dinner and we were surprised when our visitor entered before my dad had even got out of his seat. Davie Baxter was ready for a fight, but we were relieved to find it was only his tag team partner Mark Stuart.

Mark burst into the room, holding two letters aloft, one addressed to himself and one to my dad. Dad and Mark had been tag partners for five years, having met on the Scottish wrestling circuit when they were just starting out. While my dad was short, Mark Stuart was huge. He stood at about 6 foot 7 and was very muscular. He had long blonde hair and a scruffy blonde beard. Mark was incredibly strong and was able to overpower any wrestler in Britain. He wasn't technically great, but he could hold his own. His greatest strength and his greatest weakness was his battle rage. If he got angered in a match or hurt badly, he completely lost control. He would blindly attack anyone who crossed his path with no thought for their safety or his own. His power seemed to double in these moments and he felt no pain. This rage could last for a few minutes and when it had past, Mark could remember nothing of it. When he entered these rages, the opponents were normally crushed. However it often led to the Bax-Stu Boys getting disqualified after Mark had used a weapon he picked up. He would also never pin the opponent. Dad used to wait until the rage was over and he was then able to quickly settle Mark down and get him to tag. Dad would then pick up an easy victory. While Mark was in the rage, dad would do his best to hide weapons from him or stop Mark going too far. But Mark would even attack dad if he got in his way. Over the years, dad had learned how to best prevent this from happening. Sometimes an opponent would dodge Mark's mad rush and Mark would injure himself by crashing into something. It wouldn't matter while the rage was on (unless he knocked himself out), but after the rage passed Mark would suffer badly. The rage didn't happen that often, maybe about one in every ten matches. But when it did the match was soon over, one way or another.

"Aw'right Davie. Aw'right Jock ya wee numpty," Mark greeted in his thick Eastern Scottish accent. "You'll never guess what these letters are about."

"We're getting a Knighthood from the Queen for services to wrestling," my dad joked.

"No. Way better than that," Mark said, a huge beaming smile lighting up his face. "We've been invited to the World Wrestling Warriors: Fight For Your Contract show! Big Ernie Dallas sent these letters."

"To us?" dad asked, jumping to his feet. "You're joking big man. Don't joke about something like that."

"No joke," said Mark, throwing the letter to my dad. "Read it and see."

My dad tore open the letter and he couldn't believe his eyes:

Dear Mr Baxter,

You and your tag partner Mark Stuart are invited to Dallas, Texas for the W.W.W: Fight For Your Contract show. I'm sure you have heard that I am starting the W.W.W, the world's first global wrestling federation and I am looking for the best wrestlers on the planet to join. I have already signed some of the world's most famous as you will have read in the papers. But I have invited some other popular, successful and talented wrestlers to the Fight For Your Contract event. In this show, wrestlers will face off against each other and the ones who impress me will get a W.W.W contract and the opportunity to fight at the world's first ever wrestling pay-per-view, the W.W.W: Night of Warriors.

You are lucky enough to have been granted this opportunity. I've heard a lot of good things about you.

Your flights and accommodation will be arranged and paid for by us and you will be paid $1000 for wrestling at the Fight For Your Contract show. If you are successful in this show, we will discuss your long-term contract.

I look forward to seeing you in the USA,

Big Ernie Dallas: W.W.W Chairman

"Fight For Your Contract," my dad said in wonder. "The best against the best."

"Aye," Mark replied beating his chest proudly. "And we are the best."

"$1000!" I exclaimed. "You only got £40 for tonight's show dad."

"And if we do well, we can get that money every week," said Mark.

"And you could wrestle in the Big Ernie Dallas Stadium dad. Wow!"

Big Ernie was building a new stadium for the Night of Warriors pay-per-view. It was a stadium for all sport and would seat 120,000 people. A stadium that Dallas said would be "The Sporting Wonder of the World."

"Are we going dad? To America?"

"Pack your bags boy," my dad said giving me a hug.

"The land of opportunity awaits."

Chapter 2: Dallas Calling

The trip on the planes to America went on forever. I say planes because we had to fly from Edinburgh to London, to New York and finally to Dallas. It took hours.

I moaned that I was bored pretty early on, but dad had taken lots books for me to read. I said that I didn't want to read boring books, but when he gave me some football stories, I loved them. That was when my love of reading began, on those long flights to different places that my dad wrestled in. I couldn't read in the car when we drove around the UK, because if I did I got car sick. If I looked out of the window I felt ok, but if I looked at a book I might have ended up spewing on it. I actually did that to a school reader once. When I told the teacher that I hadn't read my book because I had got car sick and spewed on it she said, "I can see the pigs flying across the sky now Jock." I told her that she must be going mad and I got into a lot of trouble. But on a plane, I could read. And I grew to love it.

The W.W.W sent a car to pick us up from the airport in Dallas and it drove us to a hotel. Wow! The room was amazing. It was bigger than our caravan. We had a tv with loads of channels, so many more than at home. The beds were huge and I practised my wrestling moves on them while dad had a shower. I did an elbow drop, jumping from one bed and landing in another. Then I did a leg drop on Mr Smooth and pinned him for the 3 count. Ok. Not the real Mr Smooth. I actually leg dropped a pillow. But it was a good leg drop.

After defeating a few more famous (pillow) wrestlers, I got a bit carried away. I pulled a table closer to one of the beds, climbed onto it and attempted a moonsault onto the bed. I had never tried a moonsault before, where you stand facing away from the opponent (pillow) and jump up performing a somersault in the air landing belly first onto the opponent (pillow). My first attempt was a bit of a failure. I hit the side of the bed head first and bounced off onto the floor with a crash. Luckily I wasn't hurt badly with just a graze on my head, but I looked up to see my dad laughing down at me and I felt really silly. I did perfect the move by the end of the week though.

Another car picked us up outside the hotel and took us to Big Ernie's Wrestling Camp. It was a large building which contained three wrestling rings, Big Ernie's office and some other rooms which would later be studios for recording entrance music and wrestler's interviews for tv shows. The car driver led my dad, Mark Stuart and I straight to Big Ernie's office.

It was a large office, with signed photos of loads of legends of wrestling on the walls. There was Grappler Graham Vines, Big Vinnie Sermon, Quick Silver Smart, the Japanese legend Buzzako, Mountain Mark Tarnoli and a young Big Ernie Dallas holding the Texas Title in the air.

Big Ernie was a local legend in the state of Texas. He had played American Football for the Dallas Drivers winning three US Championships. Then he had become a wrestler and achieved success locally, then across the whole of the USA. He was respected around the world too, having had great matches in Mexico, Canada, Japan and throughout Europe. While earning good money through sport, Big Ernie had invested in oil and had made his millions. He was now putting some of this money back into his true loves; football and wrestling. He had bought the Dallas Drivers football team and now he was starting the world's first global wrestling federation, the World Wrestling Warriors. Furthermore, he was building The Big Ernie Dallas Stadium for both football and wrestling. The man who shook our hands now was a living legend.

"Howdy boys, nice to finally meet you," Big Ernie said in a loud, confident, Texas accent. "You must been Mark. Big guy like me. Nice to see. And you must be Davie. Great technician I hear. And young Jock. Nice to meet you. Strong grip too. You'll be a tough guy then. How did you get that graze on your head boy? You been fighting the local lads already huh?"

"He tried to do a moonsault off of a table onto a pillow on the bed in the hotel room," my dad said with a chuckle. "He missed."

"Oh my," Big Ernie laughed. "There goes your unbeaten record. The pillow won by count-out."

Big Ernie Dallas was in his 50s at this time. He stood at about 6 foot 5 and he was still muscular, but he did have a bit of a gut. He wore a white cowboy hat and his trademark black sunglasses that he never took off in public. His hair was a shade of light grey that could be called silver and so was his thick moustache. As always he wore a brown leather jacket, a white shirt and blue W.W.W tie, blue jeans and stylish white cowboy boots.

He had shiny white teeth fixed in what seemed to be a permanent smile. Even when he was angry he smiled, because he knew he would get what he wanted. "People listen to me because people listen to money," was a classic saying of his. "I smile because I'm rich, strong, healthy and most importantly respected. I don't need to snarl to get my message across. People will do what I want whatever, so I can afford to stay calm and happy. So I can always smile." I thought he was the most amazing man I could ever possibly meet.

"Now here's the deal boys," Big Ernie said, getting down to business after some general chit chat. "This is your big opportunity. Don't blow it. I'm building this global wrestling company and I want the best in the world. I've signed some of the world's most famous to a long-term contract already. Because of their reputation and the guaranteed money they will draw due to their popularity.

They will get paid the most too. The most successful and popular get more money. That's what you must aim for. So these long-termers are Classic Charlie Clean, Bruiser Braddock, No-Nonsense Nelmes and The Irish Champion Bert Doran. The rest of the guys, including you, have to prove themselves at the Fight For Your Contract show. Win and you get a contract. Lose, but show me you've got something and you might also get a contract. Lose and show nothing worth my time and you can go home. Got it?"

"Got it chief," Mark replied and my dad nodded.

"Chief? I like that," said Big Ernie. "Now a car will take you back to the hotel and you will meet the other guys for dinner tonight. I'm watching the football game this evening so I won't be there. Make a good impression on the other wrestlers tonight and be careful. There's some sly ones there. I'll see you in the morning for training.

Have a good night. Relax. Enjoy the big city. Dallas is the

place to be right now. "

Chapter 3: Dining With The Boys

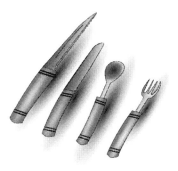

And to a ten year old Scottish lad, Dallas was an amazing place. The taxi ride at night to the restaurant in the city opened my eyes wide with wonder. Bright lights lit up the night, shining out of skyscrapers the size of which I had never seen before. I was awestruck. But meeting the wrestlers that night, would be an even more unforgettable experience.

Big Ernie's Diner was a sport themed restaurant, with big tvs showing sport on every wall beside signed photos of the world's most famous athletes from every major sport on the planet. We were the last to arrive and we felt a little intimidated as all the eyes of the long table of wrestlers turned in our direction as we approached.

"Bad enough having to sit with these talentless scum son, but those two Scottish fools belong in a circus show. Best wrestlers in the world? They're not even the best wrestlers in their rat ridden hole of a country. Waiter! Set us up another table. Come on Barry son. Let's sit somewhere else away from this shower of shame."

These words were spoken by Bruiser Brad Braddock, an English wrestler from London who we knew well. Dad held Mark back, and I was worried that the rage would take him, but Dad spoke to him calmly and Mark remained quiet. Bruiser was the best wrestler in the UK. He was big, strong and technically gifted. At 33 years of age, he stood at 6 foot 2 and weighed 280 pounds. He had small, beady blue eyes and a head shaved completely bald. His stubbly black beard failed to hide a long scar that ran down the left hand side of his face. Bruiser had won the UK Heavyweight Title three times and had won titles throughout Europe. In fact, his last reign as UK Champion had lasted four years and he had never lost the title but had given it up to come to Dallas and join the W.W.W. He was one of the wrestlers signed for a long term contract and he was a nasty mean piece of mud.

Maybe even nastier than Bruiser Brad, was his 12 year old son Barry. Dad and Mark had wrestled in the same arena as Bruiser many times, but not against him as he was a singles wrestler and they were a tag team. When they did wrestle in the same arena, I always met up with Barry and he was a bully. Two years older than me, he was big for his age with his dad's natural big frame and he loved to assert his dominance over other kids. When nobody was looking, he would punch me and kick me, put me in wrestling holds until I cried, then walked away laughing about it. When I say he did this when nobody was looking, that's not quite true. He would also do it when other kids were there and if the only adult there was his dad, who encouraged his son to be a tough guy and enjoyed watching his boy beat up other kids.

We had known that they were going to be there and we were all determined not to let them ruin this chance. So we sat together in three empty seats and joined the other wrestlers, who also seemed relieved that the Braddocks had left the table.

"Welcome guys," said a smart and athletic looking man with a smooth face and neatly slicked back black hair. "Don't let that big gorilla bother you. We're not all like that. We don't all need to hide our nerves behind a tough man persona. Most of us are confident in who we are and look forward to working with new talent like you guys. I've heard a lot of good things about you two. Nice to meet you."

"Thanks Mr Clean," my dad replied respectfully. "It is an honour to meet you."

My eyes lit up at the realisation that I was meeting the world's most famous wrestler from New York, Classic Charlie Clean. At 37, he had already had a legendary career. He was the most technically gifted wrestler in the world, arguably of all time. At 6 foot 2 and 235 pounds he was tall and well built, if not huge. But his speed, incredible number of moves, aerial ability, stamina and refusal to quit made him very difficult to beat. He was immensely popular wherever he fought and he had competed all over the world winning titles and respect. He was the world's most popular, respected and successful wrestler. It was no surprise that he was on a long term contract and all the other wrestlers at that table looked up to him. I had just met my hero.

"Nice to meet you too young fellow," he said to me. "You look like you might follow in your father's footsteps and be a wrestler one day as well. Would you like that?"

"Yes sir," I replied immediately and the thumbs up he gave me filled my heart with joy. Already, the Braddocks were forgotten.

The other two wrestlers already on long term contracts were No-Nonsense Nelmes and Bert Doran. They were two similarly dull looking individuals. Both had short unremarkable brown hair, easy to forget faces and wore clothes that I can't recall but were certainly not worth remembering. Both were 30 years old and stood at about 6 foot 3, weighing around 250 pounds. In appearance they could have been twins; except Bert Doran had a cheeky twinkle in his green Irish eyes. No-Nonsense Nelmes looked like an emotionless zombie as he slowly chewed his chicken drumstick.

Dull they may have looked, but they were both fantastic wrestlers. No-Nonsense Nelmes was Canadian and had been Canadian Champion 4 times. He too had wrestled all over the world, winning titles in South Africa and India. He was a great technician and was a master of submission.

Bert Doran had been the Irish Champion for six years until dropping the title a week ago to come to Dallas. He was strong and had good technical ability, although not as good as Nelmes let alone Classic Charlie Clean. He had also been UK Champion twice, feuding at times with Bruiser Brad Braddock. It had been a heated rivalry with

Doran causing Braddock's scar when he threw him into the ring post. Braddock had got some revenge when he won the UK Title from Doran in a cage match in Manchester, but judging by the way the two men stared at each other that night, their feud was far from over.

Another difference between two men was that Bert Doran had brought his son Larry to Dallas with him and his beautiful wife Bronwin. I had met Larry a few times before and he was a great laugh. He was ten like me and he was always up to mischief. Barry Braddock would hit him too and we had started speaking to each other by complaining about this together. Then we had grown to be friends. Larry Doran had brown hair like his dad, but the cheeky twinkle in his eyes shone far brighter than his father's. I was really pleased to see him there and it wasn't long before he was up to his usual tricks. When No-Nonsense Nelmes wasn't looking, Larry took a squeezable bottle of ketchup and quickly squished a little bit of sauce onto the napkin that Nelmes had tucked into his t-shirt. It was done so swiftly and cleverly that nobody noticed. A bit later Nelmes wiped his face with the napkin and myself and Larry barely controlled our laughter. Nelmes had a big red drop of ketchup on his nose for the rest of the meal. At least it made him look a bit more interesting.

Other wrestlers of note at Big Ernie's Diner that night were a tag team called the Idaho Invincibles, a Mexican tag team called Los Chicos Valientes who wore their wrestling masks at the table and a wrestler from New Zealand called Maximum Mike Tullis.

Maximum Mike was short for a wrestler, but he was an amazing high-flyer. He could perform all sorts of moves in the air, twisting and turning and often missing and taking himself out. I knew how that felt. He was one of the youngest there at only 27 and he was the smallest being only 5 foot 7 and weighing about 180 pounds. But he was one of the most exciting wrestlers in the world. Many questioned why he was invited to the W.W.W as his win rate was poor, but I had loved watching tapes of his matches and I was glad he was here.

I wasn't so glad to see that he had a daughter. Another 10 year old with red hair who kept grinning at both me and Larry Doran. We both ignored her. She was a girl. Like Bert Doran, Maximum Mike was here with his wife. This too upset me.

The conversation at the table was fascinating, with the wrestlers all talking about the places they'd competed in, the weird and wonderful wrestlers they'd faced and the funny things that had happened to them on their adventures.

"So there are going to be more wrestlers joining before Night Of Warriors?" Mark asked in his deep Scottish voice.

"And after," Classic replied. "There's so many great ones around the world, I'm interested to see who will appear."

"I just hope Dallas doesn't bring in Caveman Bob. He's a nightmare!" Maximum Mike exclaimed.

"Craziest guy that I ever worked with," laughed Classic, who had the best stories and everyone gave him their undivided attention when he spoke. "I've wrestled him all over, but one night in Mexico City I will never forget. Now the crowd in Mexico are a bit different. They get really into the matches. Like if you upset them or hurt their favourites, they attack you. The people in the crowd actually attack the wrestlers, especially the wild old women who hit you with their handbags. One caught me on the cheek once when I was younger and wrestling the Mexican legend El Unico. I'm sure that old woman had a brick in her bag. After that though, I earned their respect by wrestling fairly and by doing some high-flying moves. They love that in Mexico. Well this match with Caveman Bob was going ok. I was doing well and the Mexican crowd were cheering me on. But after about twenty minutes, Caveman was tiring. Desperately he threw me out of the ring, followed me out and spat on my face. Well this Mexican grandmother smacked him in the head with her bag. Caveman was furious! He looked like he was going to punch her in the face. Instead, he turned around, pointed his big backside at her and tried to force out a fart near her face. The thing is… he had had about fifteen tacos in some cheap little café before the match and they had made him feel a bit ill you know."

Everybody was giggling, waiting for the punchline.

"So what happened?" asked little Larry Doran.

"Well…Caveman Bob didn't fart. He pooped his stinking pants didn't he!"

The whole table erupted into fits of laughter.

"Still had to finish the match didn't we," Classic continued when everyone had settled down again.

"Did you win?" I asked him.

"Yeh. With a roll-up. But I sure as heck didn't pull his tights."

It was a great night, and nobody was bothered by Bruiser Braddock's rude behaviour. We got to know the guys and Dad and Mark ended the night signing Scottish folk songs. I was so excited to be here and I knew my dad and Mark were too. I really hoped they would do well at the Fight For Your Contract show. I wanted to stay here forever.

Chapter 4: Training Camp

The next few weeks were spent at Big Ernie's

Wrestling Camp, where my dad and Mark trained with the

other wrestlers in preparation for the Fight For Your

Contract show. Myself and the other wrestlers' kids went

there and did some basic school lessons with some old guy

who I can't really remember to be honest. I don't

remember much about the lessons either and I doubt

anybody wants to read about school work when they

expect to read a wrestling story. But I do remember the

other wrestlers' kids and I think people will want to read

about them because they will know they became important figures in the W.W.W history like me.

There are some things you always remember about school though. I remember that I was the best at literacy, Larry Doran was the best at art and making jokes and Barry Braddock was not bright at all. Barry hid the fact that he was poor at all school work by insulting and bullying both the other kids and the teacher. When asked a question he didn't know the answer to, he would just tell someone else to answer it or he'd smash them. He chucked pencils at us and the teacher's back and he would spit on you when the teacher wasn't looking. Basically he was a nasty bit of mud.

The best at maths was the daughter of Maximum Mike Tullis, Izzie. Looking back, she was good at everything really, but us boys didn't want to admit that. Boys didn't like girls!

We called her Firefly, because of her red hair like fire and the fact that she was small and thin. It was meant to be an insult, but I think she always liked it. It has since become such a famous name in the wrestling business that nobody would ever think it was an insult. But trust me, it was.

Firefly always buzzed around Larry and I, following us everywhere. It was understandable really. She was thousands of miles from home and to begin with there were only three other kids in Big Ernie's Wrestling Camp and one of them was muddy Barry Braddock. So we were the only possible friends she could have. But Larry and I never thought about that at the time. We just thought she was annoying and ugly. Well, we said she was ugly, but secretly we thought she was pretty. It was years later that we finally admitted that though. Boys didn't like girls.

While we were in those boring lessons, the wrestlers were training hard. They were in the gym a lot and they worked on moves in the ring with training partners and the W.W.W trainer. Whenever Larry and I had a chance, we would go to watch the training in the ring. Even though they didn't really fight each other and just practiced moves, it was amazing to watch. Classic Charlie Clean was just perfect! He could perform any move, perfectly. Bruiser Braddock was brutal. Larry told me he had a poster of him on his bedroom wall at home above his bed. I couldn't image why. It was great to see No-Nonsense Nelmes and Bert Doran in action, but the tag teams were worryingly impressive. Luckily, Dad and Mike performed well too and I was glad they didn't look out of place.

But the most fun to watch was Maximun Mike Tullis. He practiced dives out of the ring onto mats, doing somersaults mid-air. He tried all sorts of mad moves off of the turnbuckles, doing twists and turns and smashing onto the mat. It hurt him every time, but he just got up and tried some more. Firefly, who was always there when we watched, trying to discuss the wrestlers with us, kept telling her dad to stop. Maximum Mike would say something like, "No worries Izzie. I need to learn moves like this if I'm going to beat the best and get a job here."

After a few weeks at camp, Larry went over to speak to the trainer when the wrestlers had finished for the day.

"Can we have a go in the ring fella?" Larry asked in his cool Irish accent.

"This should be good. Have a go punks," the trainer said.

You may have guessed that this was the legendary wrestling trainer Stu Smith. Stu is arguably the best technical wrestler of all time. He had been a Dallas Tag Team Champion ten times, two times with Big Ernie Dallas. He would have had even more success if he had been a bit taller. He was strong, but he was only 5 foot 4 and that is really small for a wrestler. But with his knowledge of wrestling and his tough but kind and honourable personality, he was the perfect trainer.

Stu Smith had tanned skin and sharp blue eyes that I always thought could see the thoughts in my mind. He had a deep Texas accent and a gravelly voice. His gravelly voice was due to the fact that he constantly smoked cigars.

Not something an athlete would do today, but Stu was old school. He had short grey hair and bushy grey eyebrows. We knew who he was and already respected him completely.

Tentatively at first, Larry and I tried some moves in the ring. It must have looked terrible because we'd never been in a ring before. But we tried hard and Stu shouted encouragement and advice. We hurt each other a little bit, but we didn't go all in. I managed to get Larry down with a clothesline and he knocked me over with an impressive dropkick.

"Where did you learn that kid?" Stu asked.

"I practice them on a poster above my bed at home," Larry replied and I got back to my feet laughing. We were having great fun.

Until Barry Braddock turned up that is. He demanded a match with one of us, but Stu told him to let us finish our match. However, Larry stopped fighting me and glared at Barry.

"No Stu," Larry said. "No offense to you, but I want to fight that dirty piece of mud. Show him Irish spirit."

It was more like a playground fight than a wrestling match. Stu watched carefully, making sure nobody got really hurt. But he let them fight. Like I said, old school. To the older generation, boys were meant to be tough and the best way to learn toughness was to fight. These days we would never let kids fight, certainly not encourage it, but the old days were different. Having been a kid in those days, I think I'd rather have been a kid today.

It was a quick fight. Barry, two years older remember, was a lot bigger than Larry and I. Larry put up a great fight, but eventually Barry got his arm locked in an armbar and there was no escape. Larry may have quit eventually, but Stu never let it go that far.

"Ok Barry," he called. "That's it. You've won. Let him go."

Barry let go. Then he demanded his match with me.

My first professional wrestling match is famous and talked about often. This match, I have tried very hard to forget. I tried a dropkick, missed completely and landed on the back of my head. I heard Larry laugh briefly, then I felt a thump on my nose. Barry had punched me hard. Then my arm was twisted in agony and Stu again called Barry off and told him he had won.

Twenty seconds I lasted. My first match. Twenty muddy seconds.

"What a jobber! Jock The Jobber. That will be your wrestling name," Barry laughed.

A jobber is a wrestler who loses all the time.

"Enough for today boys," Stu said with a glint of sympathy in his blue eyes.

"But I want a go," Firefly moaned.

"You're not allowed to wrestle. You are just a girl," Stu replied.

"I can beat that bully Barry."

"Your job is to beat eggs. Leave this to men," said Stu.

"Can we have a go again tomorrow?" Larry asked.

"Up to you guys. I'll be here," said Stu Smith.

Hurt and embarrassed I may have been, but I went back the next day with Larry. We wrestled again, then we both got beaten up by Barry Braddock. But we still went back. I remember the look of respect in Stu Smith's eyes when he saw us turn up to wrestle every day, despite getting beaten up the time before. He began to train us a little, teaching us different holds and moves and although each session only lasted about half an hour, we learned quickly. We improved, but so did Barry. He still beat us easily every time, but we got better at somethings. We were better at bouncing off the ropes and we were better at doing moves off the top turnbuckle.

Firefly went every day as well and every day she asked Stu if she could have a go. He always said no, but the more she asked the more he smiled.

"That girl's got spirit," he would say.

After these weeks in camp, Larry and I felt like we were a part of the W.W.W and we loved it. When the Fight For Your Contract show finally arrived, our dads getting a job here mattered more than ever.

Chapter 5: Fight For Your Contract

Time seemed to fly in those first weeks in the W.W.W
and it wasn't long before I was sitting at ringside at the
Fight For Your Contract show. Dad and Mark had been
getting more and more nervous as the big day approached
and the atmosphere in the wrestling camp had changed in
the last few days. Nobody had been told who they would
face in the big show and the wrestlers had been looking at
each other differently. Anyone could have been the person
they would fight for their contract. Fight for their dream to
be a part in the first global wrestling federation.

The people on guaranteed contracts were a bit more relaxed, but they had their own career defining match in the near future. The match to be the first W.W.W World Champion had been announced to the wrestlers and it would be contested at the Night Of Warriors pay-per-view. It was going to be Classic Charlie Clean v Bruiser Braddock v No-Nonsense Nelmes in a triple threat match. There was tension between these three with the chance to create history on the line.

The other wrestler with a contract already was Larry's dad, the Irish tough guy Bert Doran. He was training seriously and he was focussed for the challenge ahead.

The event was in Dallas, in the Star Stadium which held 12,000 people and it was full. I sat next to Larry and the annoying Firefly that night, all three of us nervous for our fathers. Barry Braddock sat a few seats away, refusing to sit by us "jobbers". He enjoyed winding us up, knowing how worried we were about tonight's outcome.

"Last day for you in the U.S jobbers," he called over. "Can't wait to never see you again."

Myself and Firefly were worried he was right, but Larry just laughed at him.

"My dad's got a contract too slobby gob," Larry Doran replied. "And The Bax-Stu boys will win. So will Maximum Mike. We'll be around for a while yet."

"Mike?" Barry scoffed. "No chance. My dad's gonna kill him."

Bruiser Brad Braddock v Maximum Mike Tullis

The first match of the night was Braddock v Tullis. The difference in size between the two men was great. Braddock looked like he could break Mike's neck with ease. But Mike was so quick, so agile. He danced and flipped all over the ring, and for the first five minutes of the match Braddock couldn't catch him. Maximum Mike got in a few clotheslines, dropkicks and flying knees, but Braddock stayed on his feet. It all just seemed to anger the big man, but the crowd were cheering loudly for everything Maximum Mike did. His style was so athletic, so entertaining.

About six minutes in, Maximum Mike attempted a standing moonsault, but Braddock saw it coming and caught him mid-air. Holding him aloft like I could do to my pillow, Braddock ran across the ring and hammered

Maximum Mike onto the mat with a running powerslam.

1...2... kickout

Mike just got his shoulder up. Braddock easily picked

him up off the mat and hoisted him up into the air.

Powerbomb! This time, Mike didn't move. Braddock

could easily have pinned him then, but he wanted more

from the match. Grinning nastily, he picked him up again.

Powerbomb! The crowd booed angrily. Braddock just

laughed and picked him up again. Powerbomb! The

crowd's boos were now hurting my ears. The Bruiser put

Maximum Mike in the Brad-Lock. This was a move in

which he held his opponent's leg in the air and twisted his

ankle to the side hard. Many wrestlers had sprained and

broken their ankles in this move in the UK. Mike was

crying in pain, but he didn't quit. Slowly, agony burning

in his reddened face, he tried to crawl to the ropes. But Braddock was too strong and he pulled Mike back into the centre of the ring.

Mike had no choice. He tapped out. He had to submit. Fans often say that wrestlers should not give up, they should fight with everything that they have. But Mike's ankle could have been broken and he would have then been out of wrestling for many months. If he couldn't wrestle, he would have earned no money. How then would he support his family?

The crowd booed Braddock as he celebrated in the ring. Barry laughed at Firefly and we actually had to hold her back because she tried to climb over the chairs to fight him.

Bruiser Braddock started to leave the ring and Maximum Mike slowly got back to his feet. The crowd applauded Mike's efforts and he raised his hand to thank them. Suddenly, Braddock dashed back into the ring and violently grabbed Mike again. Powerbomb!

The crowd went crazy, booing and shouting insults and some even throwing things at Braddock in the ring. He just left the arena celebrating by flexing his muscles, laughing at the irate crowd.

"Ha ha!" laughed Barry. "My dad's gonna be the World Champion. Your dad's going home a jobber. I'm off to celebrate with my dad the winner. He's a wrestler you know. Now your dad's not by the way. Ha ha!"

We held Firefly back again and when Barry had gone, she started to sob.

"That's girls for you," I said to Larry, secretly hoping that I would not be doing the same thing by the end of the night.

There were quite a few matches that night, but I will briefly sum up the ones worth remembering. I will of course write about my dad's match in detail. Although it was not the Main Event, I will write about it last. To me, it was the Main Event.

The Idaho Invincibles beat

The Nebraska Nightmares

The Nebraska Nightmares had a great name and pretty cool entrance music, but they were terrible wrestlers. The Idaho Invincibles were tough and strong and they won easily, winning a contract.

No-Nonsense Nelmes beat Pablo Herrero

Nelmes was great technically and easily won the match. But his wrestling style was so dull, slow and full of headlocks and armbars that most of the crowd went out to get snacks. Great wrestler though, really hard to beat.

Los Chicos Valientes beat The Dallas Duo

In fairness, The Dallas Duo were old at this time, but they were seriously outclassed by the Mexican superstars. Los Chicos were fast and worked well as a team. They were high-flyers and when they hit, they hit hard. Most impressive. Los Chicos Valientes won the contracts.

Bert Doran beat Stevie Swing

Bert was similar to Nelmes, but a bit quicker. The crowd were bored again, but Bert didn't seem to care as he won easily. Stevie Swing was young and would improve with time, but that night was one he would want to forget.

Classic Charlie Clean beat Rodeo Joe

Rodeo Joe had been around for a long time and was popular throughout America. But for us, watching Classic live for the first time was an unforgettable experience. His movement was so smooth, slipping seamlessly from one move to another. The crowd cheered and clapped throughout and myself, Larry and Firefly joined in enthusiastically. Classic won with the Clean Sweep, a legsweep-neckbreaker combination move. Both wrestlers shook hands at the end and it was the match of the night.

The Bax-Stu Boys V Paul + Saul Waters

I have to be honest and say that I missed the start of this match. I was so nervous that I had to go to the toilet. I won't go into details, but let's just say, at least I never did what Caveman Bob did.

When I came back from the toilet, the match was about seven minutes in and the crowd were pretty silent. The New Jersey brothers Paul and Saul were good wrestlers and so were dad and Mark, but they were so cautious on that night. Winning meant everything and losing would be a disaster. So they didn't try any interesting moves and were more defensive that usual.

Paul + Saul were solid wrestlers, they seemed to work better as a team and dad took a lot of punishment. They tagged in and out quickly, performing lots of double-team moves. Skilfully, they also cut off the ring so dad couldn't get to big Mark to tag him in. They saw dad as the weaker wrestler, because he was so much smaller than his partner.

They obviously hadn't watched a lot of the Bax-Stu Boys matches, because this was the way things normally went. Dad may have been small, but he could take a lot of punishment. He was tough and the opponents often tired themselves out trying to wear him out while Mark stayed fresh outside the ring. If Mark did tag in, he exploded on the tiring opponents.

However, Paul + Saul were really good and dad didn't seem able to get the tag in at all. I really thought they were going to lose and worse still, it would be dad's fault.

Another quick tag and Paul + Saul did a great double team move on my poor dad. Paul picked dad up, crouched down on the mat and held him down across his knee. Saul then climbed onto the top rope and jump off hitting dad with a legdrop across his neck.

1...2... Mark broke up the pin, entering the ring and pushing Saul off of dad. The ref told him off and ordered him back to his corner and Saul pushed Mark hard. Angry now, but not raging, Mark elbowed Saul hard on the head and Saul hit the mat in pain. Then Mark went back to his corner and dad was able to crawl over and make the tag.

Big angry Mark sprinted across the ring and clotheslined Paul, sending him over the top rope and onto the floor outside the ring. He then picked up Saul so his back was pressed against his chest, his body in an upright position. Mark then threw Saul up in the air and caught both of his feet in his hands. Immediately after this, Mark ran a few steps then launched Saul across the ring, his body turning over in the air so that he landed headfirst onto the mat. The Caber Toss. That was what Mark called this move, after the Highland Games' throwing event. A caber is a trimmed tree trunk that strong men try to throw as far as they can in the classic Scottish sport. Doing this to a man was brutal. Mark calmly walked over to the unconscious Saul and pinned him.

1...2...3!

The Bax-Stu boys had won it. Dad and Mark had won the World Wrestling Warriors' contracts. I was ecstatic! Dad and Mark celebrated in the ring, hugging each other joyfully. The crowd cheered too, impressed with Mark's Caber Toss and I believe dad's toughness. They'd done it and now the adventure could really begin.

Chapter 6: Getting Over

The thing everybody wanted to know now was who would be facing who at the first ever wrestling pay-per-view, Night Of Warriors. We knew who would fight for the W.W.W World Title, but Dad and Mark were now dreaming of competing in the W.W.W World Tag Team Championship match. I was excited about this too, and I was glad that I could still train with the other kids and Stu Smith.

The day after the Fight For Your Contract show, the wrestlers gathered in the wrestling camp gym to meet Big

Ernie Dallas. Seats had been placed near one of the rings for the occasion, but there were less wrestlers than had been there previously. Many had been let go after the big show, but some who lost had been kept on for giving good performances or for showing potential. These were Rodeo Joe, Paul + Saul Waters, Stevie Swing and Maximum Mike Tullis. I was pleased to see that Maximum Mike had been kept on, but I was annoyed to find myself sitting next to Firefly again.

"More wrestlers will join before the Night Of Warriors, but the show will be mostly filled with you guys sitting here now. You truly are the world's finest wrestlers," Big Ernie began his speech in a new W.W.W shirt, tie and cowboy hat and I felt so proud that my dad was one of the men sitting there.

"Who's coming Big Ernie?" Rodeo Joe asked.

"The best," Big Ernie answered. "But I like surprises so you will find out when the time is right."

The wrestlers were quiet then. They held Big Ernie in great respect and they were interested in what he had to say about last night's show and what he expected of them at Night Of Warriors.

"Last night's show was ok," Big Ernie continued. "There were some great matches like Classic v Rodeo Joe. There were some solid matches like No-Nonsense's match and Doran's. But the crowd were quiet in those matches. To be the world's best is not just to be good technical wrestlers. It's not just winning that makes you a legend. It's creating excitement. Putting on entertaining matches. Being an entertaining character. Basically it's called getting over. The crowd should go wild when you enter the arena. I don't care if they cheer or boo or both, but they must care about everything you do in the ring. That's what makes people talk about you. That's what makes them remember you when your career is over. That's what makes you a legend. I don't want you to be just good wrestlers. I want you to be legends!"

Big Ernie Dallas's voice echoed off every wall in the room after this line and the wrestlers looked at him in awe. He was a legend and he knew what he was talking about. But most of them were not sure how they could get over because all they had thought about before was winning. But impressing him mattered. This was the opportunity of a lifetime. The biggest wrestling company, the most money, the greatest glory. Big Ernie's words were gold.

"Last night the crowd cared most about Classic and Bruiser Braddock. You guys have got it. But Nelmes and Doran! Boring. You need to learn how to perform. Get a gimmick. Play a role like an actor. If the crowd doesn't care about you, I can't sell tickets for your fights. A pay-per-view is when people pay money just for one show to be put on the tv in their homes. They won't pay money to watch boring people have boring matches. So if you don't draw money, there is no point in me paying good money for you to be here. You guys are experienced professionals so when you next fight, show me that you can entertain. Luckily for you, I've hired a film director and actor to help you to get over with the crowd. His name is Hank Tabone."

I had never seen anyone dress like Hank Tabone before and to me he looked really strange. He obviously thought a lot of his appearance as he strutted up to the wrestlers in his designer black shoes, running a hand through his slick black hair. He wore a stylish black suit and trousers, with a white flower pinned to the left side of his suite jacket.

His shirt and tie however, were outrageous. The shirt was a bright red with yellow and white flowers printed all over it. The tie was bright pink with golden butterflies and roses part of its design.

"What the heck is he wearing?" Bert Doran called out.

"You've already proved my point," Hank replied in a high pitched voice. "You have commented on my clothes because I am different. I stand out. You however Bert Doran, are easily forgotten."

Hank Tabone had been a famous film star and had recently had success in film directing. Big Ernie had paid big money to hire him for W.W.W. Nobody had ever heard of a wrestling company hiring people from the world of movies before.

"You guys listen to Hank here," Big Ernie said. "He is going to turn you all into stars."

"Ok then," said Hank. "We'll start with the Idaho Invincibles. You're now Russian."

"What?" one of the Idaho boys called out. "We're not Russian. We're from Idaho."

"No. You're Russian," said Hank. "You are big and hairy and Russian."

"Are Russians big and hairy?" asked Bert Doran.

"They are if we tell people they are. If we say you're Russian, people in America will want you to lose. So they will boo you. If we say you are from Idaho, people from Idaho will love you and nobody else will care. So you are Russian. You are the Russian Bears."

"But we don't speak Russian."

"Nobody except the Russians do. And since there is not much wrestling there, we won't go there. So anywhere else, all you have to do is babble gibberish, carry a Russian flag and people will think it's Russian."

We all thought this was a joke at first, but we soon realised that Big Ernie was serious about it. The rest of the guys then waited nervously to see what they would be. Most other changes were small, just more extravagant costumes or entrance music. Hank explained how to talk to the crowd, different ways to get them to cheer during matches or get them to boo you. He discussed doing a promo, where they would record wrestlers discussing their matches on camera to show on tv. The point of promos was to promote the match and promote the wrestlers' character. Everything the wrestlers did was to sell tickets and their character. To the wrestlers there that day, this was a whole new approach to the business.

"Tell the Scottish guys what they've to do Hank," Big Ernie said when the actor had finished his lecture.

"You two are now called The Raging Highlanders and you have to wear kilts in the ring," Hank announced.

"But I'm not from the Highlands of Scotland," Mark said passionately. "I'm from Kirkcaldy. A town in the region called Fife."

"Never heard of it," said Hank. "And that's the point. People care about places they've heard of. People have heard of the Highlands so that is where you are from. You have to fit what people expect. So if you are Russian, you drink vodka and wrestling bears is your hobby. You Raging Highlanders have haggis for breakfast, lunch and dinner and drink whisky all day. And you've to dye your hair ginger because Scottish people have ginger hair. That is your gimmick. You are traditional Highlanders. And you must all live your gimmick. Live your gimmick. If a fan sees you outside of the ring, they have to see what they expect to see from you. If they see a Highlander eating pizza, then the spell is broken. So every meal you guys have in public, has to be haggis. And if you go to a café in the afternoon, you wear kilts and drink whisky. Got it?"

"Are you serious man?" asked Mark.

"Yes Hamish," said Hank.

"Eh…My name's Mark."

"Not anymore it's not," laughed Hank. "Mark's not a famous Scottish name. Hamish is. So you are now Hamish McClan and your partner is Bruce Wallace. Named after two Scottish legends. Robert The Bruce and William Wallace."

"Cool name," said my dad. My dad Bruce Wallace that is.

"Aye you get a cool name," said Hamish McClan (Mark). "I'm muddy Hamish!"

"Now our next show is in Mexico," Big Ernie announced. "The Mexican fans are famous for being really into the matches. Really passionate. I want you to get them cheering or booing as loud as you can. Make them care! Make them love you! Make them hate you! The match I give you at Night Of Warriors depends on if you win and how the crowd react to you in Mexico. The matches higher up the card, and especially the title matches, will go to the best fighters and the wrestlers people care about. Now I want a meeting with a few guys in my office to discuss their characters with myself and Hank in private. These are special characters. You tell nobody about our plans. Like I say, I like surprises. First, No-Nonsense Nelmes, then Bert Doran and finally Hamish McClan. And remember guys. In Mexico… give me all you've got!"

Chapter 7: Mexico

In the couple of weeks before Mexico, dad and I tried to get Hamish (Mark) to tell us what had been said in the meeting with Big Ernie and Hank, but he told us he was sworn to secrecy and he said nothing. We wondered why he had been chosen for the meeting over other wrestlers and I was a bit worried that dad didn't get an individual meeting.

Those days in camp were really funny. Dad (Bruce Wallace) and Hamish McClan walked around in kilts all the time eating haggis sausages. They had both dyed their hair ginger and Hamish's ginger beard made me laugh every time I saw it. Dad had even dyed his chest hair ginger! They truly were The Raging Highlanders.

The Russian Bears found it harder to embrace their gimmick. I suppose it was easier for dad and Hamish because they were actually Scottish. The Russian Bears tried their best, but they didn't sound Russian. Sadly, their attempts to learn the Russian National Anthem were awful. When they sang, it sounded like a cat drowning in a toilet. But they wore red jackets with the Russian flag on and carried the Russian flag everywhere they went. They were desperate to impress Big Ernie.

No-Nonsense Nelmes and Bert Doran practiced in a room away from the boys. I guess Big Ernie wanted their change to be a surprise. We only saw them looking the way they had always looked, which was a bit dull. Larry

Doran had no idea what his dad's gimmick was going to be and he couldn't wait until Mexico.

Us kids continued our training with Stu Smith. Larry and I also practiced gimmicks. We were Highlanders, demons, robbers, monsters, cowboys, zombies and even cavemen like that wrestler Caveman Bob we had heard about. Barry Braddock told us we were stupid, but we didn't care. It was great fun! We learned and improved a lot, but Barry still beat us easily. To Larry and I it was a bit of a game, not a real fight. We didn't really hurt each other. Barry did hurt though.

We travelled down to Mexico a week before the event and it was a culture shock. Mexico City was huge! Full of cars and people. The food was different, the language, the music, the clothes people wore and we would soon find out that the wrestling was different too. We stayed in a hotel that had a private gym and room with a ring for the guys to train in. I loved every minute of it there. I have always loved different cultures. Us kids still got school lessons with our travelling teacher, but again, they are not interesting. What happened in the Mexico show is.

The arena was special. It was called El Estadio Mexico and it was the largest purpose built wrestling stadium in the world, with 16,000 bright red seats. It had once held the boxing at the Olympic Games and all the legends of Mexican wrestling had made memories there. I sat with Larry and Firefly of course, hoping that our dads would make memories there too. However, with The Raging Highlanders up against the Mexican heroes and talented duo Los Chicos Valientes. I was once again a nervous wreck.

We sat at ringside next to Barry Braddock and some excited old Mexican ladies. The arena was full. Mexicans loved all kinds of wrestling, but they had really come to see the Main Event. It was to be Mexican Champion El Lobo Negro v Classic Charlie Clean. The match wasn't for the title, but it was two legends of the sport squaring-off so the whole of Mexico was excited.

Bruiser Brad Braddock v El Pajaro Rojo

El Pajaro Rojo was a local Mexican wrestler who wore a red mask. The wrestling mask is sacred in Mexico. Masks are a huge part of the country's culture, historically dating back to the Aztecs. Wearing a mask gives a wrestler a sense of mystery, and people love them. In Mexico, masked wrestlers even wear their masks in public. Because masks are so important, losing one to an opponent is the ultimate insult. Wrestlers have mask v mask matches, with the loser having to take off their mask and tell the crowd their real name. After this happens, they can never wear that mask again.

We couldn't believe the noise of the crowd when El Pajaro Rojo entered the arena wearing a red and gold mask. They went wild! And he wasn't even a big star. The fans were so passionate. They clapped respectfully for Bruiser Braddock, a wrestler unknown to them.

They didn't clap for long. As soon as the bell rang, Braddock hit El Pajaro Rojo with a low-blow, forcing him to bend over in pain. The crowd booed like mad. The old woman next to me actually tried to spit on Braddock, but she misfired and the slobby spit just dribbled down her chin. Braddock picked El Pajaro up and POWERBOMB!

It was the hardest powerbomb I had ever seen. Boom! El Pajaro crashed into the mat.

The crowd were incensed when Braddock didn't go for the 3 count there and then, but picked El Pajaro up again. POWERBOMB! The crowd erupted in angry shouts once more and Braddock stood in the centre of the ring and laughed at the fallen El Pajaro. Young Barry Braddock laughed too and the old Mexican ladies turned on him, shouting furiously in Spanish. He just sat there looking at them and laughing even harder.

Once again Bruiser Braddock picked up his opponent and POWERBOMB!

1…2… but Braddock pulled his lifeless opponent up again.

Security guards were now having to hold some people in the crowd back as they were trying to climb the barriers to get at Braddock. Still laughing, Braddock picked up El Pajaro Rojo one more time for a powerbomb, but then just placed him back onto his feet and held him steady with one hand, so that El Pajaro was standing up. Slap! Braddock actually softly slapped El Pajaro on the face and he fell over in a heap.

1...2...3!

Braddock finished the match with a slap. It was such an insult to a fellow professional. The crowd were stamping their feet, throwing litter in the ring and some had now actually climbed over the barriers and security were wrestling them as they tried to get into the ring. It looked like there was going to be a riot and it was just the first match.

Then Bruiser Braddock did something almost criminal. He grabbed El Pajaro Rojo's red mask and ripped it off!

This time the crowd turned silent in shock. The only noise was that of Bruiser Braddock and little Barry Braddock laughing. Suddenly, the old woman next to Barry spun around and smacked him in the face with her handbag. Reacting quickly Barry left the arena, turning his face away so we could not see the tears. Security escorted Bruiser Braddock out of the ring and into the back, fans trying to punch him and litter flying at his head all the way out of the arena.

Dejected, El Pajaro Rojo got to his feet, maskless, his head hanging in shame. He told the crowd his real name and left the arena to silence. He would never be El Pajaro Rojo again.

Luckily, the next matches calmed the crowd's anger and they started to enjoy the event.

Maximum Mike Tullis beat Stevie Swing

This was a great high-flying match and the crowd loved it. Both wrestlers got a standing applause at the end and Firefly ran into the ring and hugged her dad.

The Russian Bears beat Paul + Saul Waters

The Russian Bears came down to the ring in their red jackets holding the Russian flag and got booed. They then took the microphone and addressed the crowd.

"We are Russian," said Igor (one of their new names). Then he said it in Spanish, "Somos rusos."

After the boos had died down Vlad took the mic (the other guy's new name), and tried to speak in Russian.

"Badooshki labashi Mexico," he shouted in what was most certainly gibberish, but he said it in a negative way and the crowd listened tensely. "Ramboda hookee hookee Russia!"

This time Vlad roared enthusiastically and the Russian Bears waved the flag in the air. The crowd booed and stamped their feet in anger. We couldn't believe it. It was working.

Then they tried to sing the Russian Anthem. It was lucky for them that the crowd booed so loudly that you couldn't hear them, because they still didn't actually know the words.

The Russian Bears won a solid match, the crowd angry throughout.

"I hope my dad and Hamish can match that," I said to Larry, hoping that The Raging Highlanders would get the Tag Team Title shot at Night Of Warriors.

Sheriff Nelmes beat Maximo Torres

No-Nonsense Nelmes had become a sheriff. He slowly walked down to ringside dressed in a sheriff's outfit, black hat on his head and silver star on his shirt. In the ring he took the microphone and unenthusiastically said, "I am Sheriff Nelmes. If any of you break the law, I will arrest you. I don't like people who break the law. And don't steal my hat. It is a nice hat. Nicer than yours."

The crowd looked at him in confusion as he took off his hat and waited for his opponent.

"Is that it?" Firefly asked.

The match was dull and Sheriff Nelmes won easily. The crowd didn't care.

"I'm sure my dad can do better than that," laughed Larry.

'The Extra-Bert' Bleary O'Leary beat Rodeo Joe

Larry's dad, Bert Doran, was announced as 'The Extra Bert' Bleary O'Leary. He walked down the entrance ramp to traditional Irish fiddle music. He was wearing a long bright green jacket, black shoes with a golden buckle, green wrestling tights and a green top hat. Bright red hair stuck out of his hat and he was beginning to grow a red beard. Dyed of course.

"What on Earth is he doing?" asked Firefly.

"Getting over," laughed Larry.

Bleary O'Leary carried a green bag and he was taking some silver dust out of it and sprinkling it on the crowd. It was an incredible transformation from the serious wrestler he had been before.

"Have you seen any rainbows?" he asked the crowd when he got the mic in the ring. "I'm looking for a pot of gold now."

Most of the crowd didn't understand him, but they cheered when he did a cartwheel and blew some silver dust on the bald ref's face saying, "That's magic Irish lucky dust. It will give you good luck. Maybe you'll find a wife tonight ref. Or maybe your hair will fly off of your bum and grow back on your head."

"Irish lucky dust?" I asked my Irish friend.

"There's no such thing Jock," laughed Larry.

It was a great match! Rodeo Joe was popular in Mexico, having wrestled there many times before. And the crowd loved Bleary O'Leary (Bert Doran) and his antics. It was an even battle and neither wrestler could beat their opponent. They both refused to give up and the crowd loved it. Bleary finally won when he went up to the top rope to try a moonsault, something Bert Doran had never done. Before he jumped, he took his little green bag out of his green tights and sprinkled some magic Irish lucky dust onto his own head. Then he delivered a perfect moonsault.

1...2...3!

A great victory! A wonderful match! The crowd cheered for both men who shook hands. Larry and I were so happy we hugged each other. Larry even gave Firefly a high-five.

Los Chicos Valientes V The Raging Highlanders

It was amazing that my dad and Hamish were getting to go on second last and the crowd were hot. Los Chicos Valientes were Mexican stars, 5 time Mexican Tag Champions and 1 time Texas Tag Champs. Their names were Poderoso and Elastico and even before any of the teams had entered the arena, the crowd were singing and stamping their feet. The old ladies next to us were standing up and clapping their hands, joining in the Spanish songs that we couldn't understand. We decided to stay quiet, not wanting to get into trouble like Barry Braddock. And I was worried about what Hamish McClan was going to do after his meeting with Big Ernie. I was right to be worried.

The Raging Highlanders entered first, bagpipe music blaring. They had their kilts on, were wearing big black boots and they were both munching on a huge haggis sausage. You could tell the crowd were interested by the fact that they were perched on the edge of their seats, but they didn't know whether to cheer or boo yet. That all changed when Hamish McClan spoke into the microphone.

"You ref," he called to the referee. "Translate what I say."

Luckily the ref spoke Spanish and English and was able to translate what Hamish said word for word.

"We're from the Highlands of Scotland and this is our first time in Mexico," Hamish began then waited for the translation. "I love the wrestling masks here."

The crowd cheered after this was translated.

"I only wish you'd put the masks on your women's faces. Man, they are ugly!"

When this was translated, the crowd went mad with anger. Larry and I looked at each other in shock and even dad looked surprised in the ring.

When Los Chicos Valientes hit the ring, the crowd cheered louder than ever and the noise just got louder as the match went on. Whether Hamish was in the ring, or on the apron while dad wrestled, he made faces at the crowd. He even took a bite of haggis sausage and spat it into Poderoso's face. He was disgusting!

It was an even match, with the Mexican's high-flying style working at times, but the stronger Scottish wrestlers often over-powering them. Unlike the previous match, dad and Hamish tagged in and out regularly, but Los Chicos tagged faster and as the match went on, they seemed stronger. Hamish especially tired and he was trying rasher moves, going for wild swings and mostly missing as the speedy Mexicans dodged easily.

The long, competitive match ended suddenly. Hamish and Elastico were brawling outside the ring and Hamish was really tired now. He went for a big clothesline, but Elastico duked under it and Hamish crashed into the barriers next to us spilling the old ladies' cups of drink all over them. One angry old lady turned red in the face and grabbed Hamish by his ginger beard, pulling him towards her.

"Grosero!" she screamed into his face and smacked him with her handbag. When Hamish finally got free, he turned around and was hit in the face with a dropkick by Elastico.

RAGE! Hamish should have been hurt, but his head never even budged from the dropkick. The rage had taken over. He swatted Elastico down with a hard punch, then turned and grabbed the old lady's bag from her. Turning back to Elastico, he hammered him with the bag over and over. Poderoso ran over to help his partner and hit Hamish with a flying elbow. Hamish didn't seem to notice. He just picked up Poderoso and slammed him onto the barriers by the old woman. Elastico crawled back into the ring and dad ran over to Hamish to try to calm him down. Hamish just pushed dad over and turned back to Poderoso, picking him off the floor.

Caber Toss!

Hamish launched Poderoso over the barrier and head first into the crowd. He actually flew over our heads and landed somewhere in between rows 5 and 6! He was unconscious.

The bell rang as medics rushed to Poderoso's aid. Luckily, we later found out, he wasn't badly injured. The ref declared that Los Chicos Valientes had won the match because Hamish had been counted-out. Still in the rage, Hamish ran back into the ring after Elastico. Elastico jumped over the ropes and escaped and the ref tried to hold Hamish back, preventing him from chasing Elastico. Caber Toss!

To the ref! Security surrounded the ring and dad grabbed Hamish in a bearhug. It appeared that the rage was wearing off as Hamish's shoulders slumped. Dad and security led Hamish out of the arena and the crowd booed them madly all the way.

We couldn't believe it! Attacking a ref! Insulting the Mexicans! What a disgrace! What had happened to Hamish? The crowd were still booing long after The Raging Highlanders had left ringside. I remember sitting quietly in my seat, glad that my hair wasn't ginger.

The main event match was one of the best matches I've witnessed in my whole life, but even when watching that, I couldn't get Hamish's crazy behaviour out of my head.

Classic Charlie Clean beat El Lobo Negro

This classic wrestling match sent the crowd home happy and it was so important that it did after The Raging Highlanders had upset them so much. El Lobo Negro, which was Spanish for The Black Wolf, was one of the greatest Mexican wrestlers of all time. He was a 6 time Mexican Champion and he currently held the belt too. He was the most popular sportsman in the country and the crowd's cheering nearly lifted the roof off the stadium, and this was before he'd even come to ringside. He always wrestled in a black mask with yellow around his eyes and red around his mouth. A few people in the crowd were also wearing replicas of this mask. Classic Charlie Clean was also popular in Mexico. He had actually won the Mexican Title once and had lost it to El Lobo Negro. This non-title match was a classic battle for honour between two living legends.

They wrestled for 40 minutes, evenly matched, both men mixing different wrestling styles. Because they had both wrestled around the world they could effectively wrestle the styles of America, Mexico, Europe and Japan. It was a joy to watch. The crowd applauded and cheered every move and the wrestlers fought fair and clean.

In the end El Lobo Negro, the older of the two legends, tired and Classic capitalised on a mistake. El Lobo jumped off the top rope, attempting a high cross body, but Classic read the move. He leaped up gracefully, meeting El Lobo in mid-air and connected with a flying knee to his head.

1...2...3!

Classic Charlie Clean had won! He had avenged his loss to El Lobo Negro years ago. But he didn't celebrate. The first thing he did after the three count was help El Lobo Negro to his feet and check he was ok. When he realised that he was, Classic raised El Lobo's hand and then the two legends hugged in the middle of the ring. The crowd celebrated with them. It was an amazing end to the night.

When the wrestlers had left the ring and the crowd started to leave, Larry and Firefly talked excitedly about their dads' performances. I however, worried about

Hamish's actions. What was Big Ernie going to say?

Chapter 8: The Big Ernie Dallas Stadium

"Amazing," Big Ernie cheered. "Did you hear the crowd? Some of your performances were amazing. Bruiser Braddock! 'The Extra-Bert' Bleary O'Leary! Classic Charlie Clean! And The Raging Highlanders! All of you were superstars! The noise of the crowd was amazing. They really cared. Loved you or hated you, they felt real emotion and that's what wrestling is really about. And some of you other guys were great too. Exactly what Hank, Stu and I were looking for."

We were sitting in The Big Ernie Dallas Stadium watching Big Ernie, Stu Smith and Hank Tabone address us as they stood in the ring itself. The ring had W.W.W logos on the mat, ring apron and turnbuckles. Everything was ready for the Night Of Warriors pay-per-view. The stadium was unbelievable. And it felt special even without any fans in attendance. 120,000 seats! I tried to imagine it full and couldn't. El Estadio Mexico was the biggest stadium I'd ever been in and that was only 16,000 seats. And that had seemed huge to me. The Big Ernie Dallas Stadium was colossal.

"Next up: Night Of Warriors," Big Ernie continued. "Before we do that we're gonna record some promos to put on t.v. We've got to raise awareness and interest in the matches. So you'll be playing your characters on tv and saying how much you want to win your fight, or beat up your opponent. Whatever sells the story best."

I was relieved that he'd liked what dad and Hamish had done in Mexico. Surprised they didn't get the sack for it, but pleased. The wrestlers were waiting as patiently as they could, desperate to hear who would face who at Night Of Warriors.

"Before I tell you the matches for our big event," Big Ernie said, enjoying the tension in the room. "Let me introduce two new wrestlers we've signed. First, El Lobo Negro."

El Lobo Negro, in his trademark black mask, walked down the entrance ramp and joined the other wrestlers, shaking their hands and hugging Classic Charlie Clean.

"And our second new signing: Moldaron!"

The monster who walked down to the ring was massive. He stood at 6:10 and was about 390 pounds of muscle. He wore black tights, black boots and a white mask with black around the eyes and mouth giving it the appearance of a demonic skeleton. None of the other wrestlers had seen this character before and none had met a man of that stature in any ring anywhere in the world. He made Hamish McClan look small and he was 6 foot 7. He walked slowly down to the ring, not looking at anybody and sat away from the other wrestlers.

"Now that's a character," Big Ernie laughed. "So. Now to the matches for Night Of Warriors:

* Maximum Mike Tullis v Moldaron

* The Russian Bears v Paul + Saul Waters (Flag Match)

* Stevie Swing v El Lobo Negro

* W.W.W World Tag Team Titles Match:

Los Chicos Valientes v The Raging Highlanders

* Nelmes v Rodeo Joe

* W.W.W World Title Match

Classic Charlie Clean v

Bruiser Braddock v

'The Extra Bert' Bleary O'Leary

Now we've got to get to work promoting these matches."

"But I thought I was in the title match," said a confused looking No-Nonsense Nelmes.

"Are you kidding Nelmes?" said Hank Tabone. "You were a terrible sheriff. The crowd don't care about you. The title match has to be the match the crowd are most excited about. There's no way a bore like you can be in it."

"That's sadly right Nelmes," Big Ernie agreed. "Watching your act was about as entertaining as it would be to watch a slug doing ballet. You're a great wrestler. We just have to find a character that suits you. Look at Bleary O'Leary here. He was dull and now he is a hell of a character, who the crowd loved to watch. So he gets the title match."

Larry grinned, proud of his dad who was sitting next to him, looking like a giant drunk leprechaun.

"So for Night Of Warriors Nelmes, you are going to be Nightmare Nelmes. You'll wear red face paint, a black cape and vampire teeth. You have to scare people. Ok?"

The eternally awkward Nelmes looked totally bewildered and the other wrestlers were trying really hard not to laugh.

It was amazing. My dad and Hamish, The Raging Highlanders, had a chance to be the first ever World Wrestling Warriors World Tag Team Champions. After the match in Mexico, Dad had asked Hamish why he had

insulted the Mexicans and he had said that Big Ernie had

told him to do it to 'get over'. He'd felt bad saying those

things, but it had got them a title shot. Dad understood, but

wasn't sure he'd have done the same himself. Big Ernie

not letting dad in on the plan was just his way. He loved to

shock people, the crowd, the commentators and the

wrestlers themselves. He felt it made the shows more real

if only a few people knew some of his surprises. Even in

these early days, he was also worried that if too many

people knew his plans, somebody would leak them to the

public and ruin the surprise for everybody. Therefore, the

W.W.W was always a secretive company.

"So now we get to work," Big Ernie concluded. "Hank

will help you film your promos and Stu will train you hard

for the big night. It's coming boys. The biggest wrestling event of all time. The biggest night of your careers. The Night Of Warriors!"

Chapter 9: Selling The Night Of Warriors

We had moved to a purpose built hotel right next to the stadium so that the wrestlers could quickly get to the arena. The promos were practised then recorded in purpose built studio rooms in the stadium and the wrestling training all happened in the stadium ring itself. The guys were given allotted times for their training and promos and the rest of the time they spent in the hotel gym, pool or just relaxing.

Us kids however, still had to go to school with that one boring teacher in a studio converted into a classroom. What made it worse, was that the trainer Stu Smith was too busy to teach us wrestling and the ring was always in use, so what should have been the most exciting days ever, were actually really boring.

Another kid had joined us too. A near 6 foot twelve year old called Bor. That was his name. Just Bor. He was Moladron's boy. His dad had never spoken since his dramatic arrival and neither had his son Bor. I was intimidated by him, but he stayed out of our way at first.

The only fun we had in those days leading up to Night Of Warriors was sneaking around near the studios and listening in through the door when wrestlers were practicing their promos. These promos when ready, were being played on t.v as adverts for the event. Here are some of the things we heard, much of which were never shown on t.v:

Bruce Wallace (Dad):

In Scotland, we don't give baby boys milk. We give them whisky to bring them up tough. Milk is for cows. Whisky is for men.

Hamish McClan:

When The Tartan Rage surrounds, you're going down!

Igor (Russian Bear):

Boogla doogla vodka shivnov bivnov Kremlin Kick diznovski! Did that sound Russian?

Vlad (Russian Bear):

USA govnavos! Kremlin Kick Waters ahhh!

'The Extra Bert' Bleary O'Leary:

I'm following a rainbow and the end of it is in Dallas. In The Big Ernie Dallas Stadium. And it's there that I'll find my pot of gold when I win the W.W.W World Title.

Nightmare Nelmes:

I'm Nightmare Nelmes and even cats are scared of me. Ooooooooh. Go away cat. I'm going to pull your tail cat. Ahh come on. This is stupid!

Classic Charlie Clean:

To be the first W.W.W World Champion, in the greatest stadium in the world, would be the crowning achievement of my career. I hope you can be there with me. I will give you my all. Together, we can make history.

Bruiser Brad Braddock:

I'm not here to entertain. I'm here to win. To win the W.W.W World Title. I don't care if you buy the pay-per-view or not. I don't care about you. I care only about me. About me becoming the world champion.

I had had a chat with my dad about him and Hamish being The Raging Highlanders. Dad had told me about a conversation they'd had with Big Ernie who thought that the crowd would be more likely to boo them. Big Ernie had said that since Hamish had the battle rage, that would make him naturally bad, even if he couldn't control it. So dad and Hamish had to try to get the crowd to hate them as much as they could. Dad had seemed a little uneasy about this, but he'd told me it was all part of being in the W.W.W and I knew that dad and Hamish were good guys in our real life. But it took us all a while to get used to the fact that in the W.W.W, real life and ring life were often quite separate things.

Sadly, my moments of real life with dad were brief, because he had to play his ring character in public. Just as Big Ernie had told him to do, he wore a kilt every time he left the hotel room. All the other wrestlers stayed in character too so when we were all in public together we looked like a travelling circus.

I'll never forget one time when I went with Larry and Firefly for lunch in a café near the stadium one afternoon. There were quite a few wrestlers in there and they were all trying to remain in character. Hank Tabone was sitting at a table in the centre of the room, dressed in a pink suite, white shirt and pink leather tie. He was watching the wrestlers and they all knew that he would report their behaviour to Big Ernie.

Dad and Hamish were sitting together, wearing kilts of course. They were drinking whisky and complaining to the waitress about the food.

"Why don't you have haggis woman?" Hamish asked.

"It's not something I've heard of to be honest," she replied.

"It's a wee hairy beast that has two legs shorter than the other two so it can run up hills," dad explained.

"Oh," said a confused waitress. "Well I'm afraid we don't serve that."

"You got any pig lungs or sheep stomach then woman?" a frustrated Hamish asked.

I wasn't allowed to sit next to dad and Hamish, because they were supposed to be bad guys and bad guys didn't have lunch with kids. In the end they both ordered steak. That was one of the easiest orders for the poor waitress. Serving The Russian Bears was near impossible.

"Boogodva prashneetov kooloo kooloo coffee black," Vlad ordered.

"I'm sorry. Could you repeat that please?" the waitress asked.

"Boogoo doogoo black coffee! Ahhh! Nastrovee coffee," Vlad said in an annoyed voice. There was no way that he could ever repeat anything he had said in his false Russian.

"Black coffee? Is that right?"

"Da. Yes Yes da."

"And for you sir?" she asked Igor.

"Lemonade opeely da da."

It was easier for the 'good' guys who had more normal characters, but poor Nightmare Nelmes was really struggling. He had a long black cape on and he had his hood up, hiding most of his face. We saw that he had red face paint on, but we weren't sure if he actually had any Vampire teeth.

"Would you like to order sir?" the waitress asked him timidly.

"Steak," Nelmes mumbled. "Not a wooden one."

"Well how would you like your steak done sir?"

"Well done."

At this point, Hank Tabone drew a deep breath attracting the attention of Nelmes and reminding him to stay in character.

"I mean bloody. I want blood dripping off my meat. I love blood. Death to the cow." Nightmare Nelmes said with no enthusiasm.

I loved seeing the wrestlers in public and going for lunch at the same time as them was always entertaining.

One day in our tedious lessons, Larry and I entered the class to find Bor sitting next to Barry Braddock. Barry was talking to him and although Bor didn't say anything back, he appeared to be listening. And this went on throughout the lesson. We were supposed to be writing about our hobbies or something, but we were constantly distracted by the things Barry was saying to Bor:

"The Raging Highlanders got the title match because Big Ernie wants Los Chicos Valientes to be his first tag champs so he set them up against a weak team."

"Bleary O'Leary. What a fool! Putting him in the World Title match was a mistake."

"Your dad Moldaron is gonna destroy that skinny Maximum Mike. End his career. He won't even be able to walk again."

"You shut up!" Firefly shouted, standing up and confronting Barry Braddock. She was shaking with anger. It was obvious that she was really worried about her dad having this match with Moldaron. She had been really quiet and went straight back to the hotel after lessons. I was happy to see less of her.

"Don't be so rude to Bor here. Just because he doesn't talk, doesn't mean he doesn't have feelings. Telling him to 'shut up'. Sarcasm people call that. Well I call it rude," said Barry. "Well I'll be rude back Firefly. Your dad is going to be broken."

"Enough Braddock," Larry roared. "Pick on somebody your own size."

"What? Like you? You're not my size you little leprechaun."

"I'll put you down Braddock," Larry countered.

"Ok. Prove it."

"We'll meet you in the ring," I said. I've no idea why I said this. It just came out.

"You serious?" Barry scoffed. "Jock Jobber Baxter + Laughable Larry Doran v Barry Braddock and Bor. You're on!"

And so it was arranged. Larry and I were going to actually fight against these two bigger lads. Although the idea scared me witless, I would never back down. I could never be a coward. So the night before Night Of Warriors, when all the wrestlers had gone to bed, we snuck out of our rooms and went back to The Big Ernie Dallas Stadium. We climbed through a window we had left open in the classroom, and we were in.

It was a strange feeling wrestling a tag match in that ring, surrounded by 120,000 empty seats. We had put on some lights so that only the ring was lit up. I was scared, but excited. And the adrenaline in my body made me perform better. Larry and I knew we couldn't match Barry and Bor for strength, so we tried to mimic the Mexican style and that of Maximum Mike Tullis. We were fast, performing jumping attacks and when they attacked us, we did rolls and slides to avoid them. It worked well and we got a few good shots in, even if we didn't put either of them down.

We had decided to referee ourselves, and both teams were fair when we went for a cover. Barry may have been a nasty kid, but he respected wrestling.

Luckily, big and strong as he was, Bor was slow and had had no training. So he was easily avoided. Barry nearly got us a couple of times, but we managed to survive at first.

But we tired. Eventually, Bor caught Larry with a big hard punch to the side of the head and Larry flew across the ring. Bor walked over to pick him up, and I tagged Larry's back without Bor seeing. Bor dragged Larry across the ring, not hearing Barry telling him about my tag. Quickly, I climbed into the ring and sprinted over to Bor. Just before I reached him, I sprang into the air and delivered a cracking dropkick to the back of his head. I couldn't believe I had managed to kick that high! Bor's head shot forward and he slammed it into the turnbuckle. He was down!

Without pausing to think, I climbed up onto the top turnbuckle and went to do a moonsault. I still have a visual image in my mind today of my body turning over in the air. I had practiced a few more times on my pillow and I knew that this was perfect. It felt fantastic.

Crunch! I felt agony in my ribs as I landed on Bor's raised knees. He had pulled his knees up at the last minute and I had crashed into them. I was winded and I was worried I'd broken some ribs. For a moment, I couldn't even breathe.

Bor tagged Barry Braddock in and he put me in the Brad-Lock. When I was finally able to breathe again, I submitted.

"Not bad boys. Not bad at all," Big Ernie's voice called from somewhere in the dark stadium. He then walked down the steps and entered the ring, helping me to my feet. "Nice moonsault. You were unlucky. Should have sprinkled some Irish Lucky Dust on your head before you jumped."

We looked at Big Ernie, wondering when he would start shouting at us for sneaking in and using his ring.

"Now get off to bed boys," he said. "Don't let me catch you wrestling here again. It's your dads' turn tomorrow and I can't wait."

We did go home after that. But before we went to bed, we arranged a rematch for tomorrow night after Night Of Warriors.

Chapter 10: Night Of Warriors

The event was a sell-out, 120,000 people filled the new stadium, cheering as Big Ernie Dallas walked into the ring. He addressed the crowd, telling them how happy he was that they had joined him in this historic moment, the world's first wrestling pay-per-view. The true beginning of the World Wrestling Warriors federation started that night. The first World Champion and Tag Team World Champions were crowned, and I was sitting with Larry Doran and Firefly in the front row.

Barry Braddock and Bor sat at a different side of the ring, so they didn't really bother us during the event. But we did stare at each other from time to time, remembering the fight we had arranged in that very ring for later in the night. However, we rarely looked their way because the action in the ring was so exciting. We were truly living wrestling history.

Maximum Mike Tullis v Moldaron

The crowd cheered Maximum Mike when he came to the ring. The matches at the Fight For Your Contract show and in Mexico had been repeatedly shown on tv as had the promos. People already liked Maximum Mike from what they'd seen on tv. It was going to be interesting to see how this new audience reacted to the wrestlers after watching them on tv. Some wrestlers like Classic Charlie Clean and Rodeo Joe they already knew well, others they'd only seen recently on the telly. Some they would react to as soon as they saw them, like Maximum Mike, others they would hardly cheer or boo when they entered. Those guys had to use this huge event to make people interested in them, to get over.

Moldaron was one of those guys. The crowd had hardly seen him at all. In his promos he just looked at the camera, never speaking. He had never wrestled as far as any of us knew. He entered the arena to booming music and people were immediately drawn to his size.

"Look at the size of that monster!" one guy exclaimed behind me.

Moldaron was massive, and he looked even bigger standing next to little Maximum Mike. It was a quick match.

Maximum Mike darted around the ring, dodging big slow Moldaron punches and trying a few flying elbows, knees and dropkicks. He hit Moldaron many times, but

Moldaron never even budged when he got hit. He just stared at Maximum Mike and went to attack again.

Eventually, Moldaron connected with a giant clothesline. Maxiumum Mike's body did a 360 degree spin in the air and he landed hard on the back of his neck.

"Ooooohhh!" the whole crowd seemed to cry in unison.

Bending down, Moldaron picked Maximum Mike up like he weighed nothing at all and lifted him into the air above with his two hands. He then quickly raised his two arms into the air, like a weightlifter performing a jerk lift. Except instead of holding Maximum Mike up in the air, when his arms reached their highest, Moldaron let go of Mike and threw him up above his head. Mike's body seemed to float for a second and then he tumbled back towards the mat. But Moldaron didn't let him fall for long. As Maximum Mike was dropping, Moldaron himself jumped up and hit Mike with an uppercut to the jaw. This move was later named The Power Cut. It was the most devastating move I had ever seen. And Maximum Mike Tullis was completely unconscious.

Firefly screamed and tried to climb the barriers to get to her dad. Larry and I actually had to hold her back. Fortunately, Moldaron did not appear to be as vicious as Bruiser Braddock. He calmly covered Maximum Mike.

1..2..3!

The crowd mostly booed, but some cheered. It was hard not to be impressed with Moldaron's size and power. He left the ring and luckily Maximum Mike was able to get back to his feet with the help of some medics. It was an interesting way to start the biggest ever wrestling show and the crowd were already fully engaged.

The Russian Bears v Paul + Saul Waters

(Flag Match)

The crowd didn't really react to the American team of Paul + Saul, but The Russian Bears got heavily booed when they entered the arena with the Russian flag. I felt a bit sorry for the two guys from Idaho as people chanted, 'U.S.A' at them.

"Shpaduknee golodov America ptarod!" Igor cried before spitting on the mat. The crowd went nuts, booing like crazy. They were so insulted by what he had said about America, which I knew was just made up garbage words.

"Russia shpatnee America!" Vlad shouted to even greater boos and litter started to fly into the ring, the crowd now throwing things at The Russian Bears in anger. "Now we sing Russian National Anthem."

Paul +Saul stopped this by attacking The Russian Bears and this time they got a cheer. The match had started.

In a flag match like this, on one turnbuckle the American flag was tied to the top of a pole and on another one a Russian flag was tied. The first team to get their country's flag down was the winner.

It was a bit of a messy match to be honest, but the crowd enjoyed it. It seemed that Big Ernie was right when he said that people caring about characters was at least as important as the actual wrestling.

The Russian Bears got their flag first and won, but Paul + Saul got the American flag after the match and attacked the Russians with it. Paul hit Igor with the flag, sending him out of the ring over the top rope. Then he chucked the flag to Saul, who did the same thing to Vlad. It seemed to make them bad losers to me. I mean they had attacked The

Russian bears before the match started and again at the end when they had lost. However, the crowd seemed to love them for it. Nevertheless, both teams left looking strong and with the crowd more interested in their characters so I guess the match was a success.

Stevie Swing v El Lobo Negro

Young Stevie never got any reaction when he came in, but El Lobo Negro got a big cheer. He had wrestled in Dallas many times before, and people had loved watching the match between him and Classic in Mexico.

This was another great match. At 40 years old, El Lobo was maybe just past his best at this stage in his career, but he was still in amazing shape. Stevie was at the start of his wrestling journey at just 23 years old, but for 15 minutes he matched El Lobo move for move. El Lobo's experience really helped the young guys in W.W.W develop in those first years. Everyone who spent time in the ring with him, came out a better wrestler.

After about 20 minutes, El Lobo Negro hit Stevie Swing with a high-cross body off the top rope.

1..2..3!

Both men shook hands at the end and both men were cheered loudly by the crowd. Another successful match.

W.W.W Tag Team Championship Match:

Los Chicos Valientes v The Raging Highlanders

This was it. The one I had been so nervously waiting for. Despite Big Ernie making them 'bad guys, I had still hoped that dad and Hamish would get cheered, but they received the loudest boo of the night so far. I was really upset with this, but when dad walked past me he smiled and winked, so I felt better knowing that he was ok with it. They were certainly getting a reaction! People had seen the promos and the Mexican fight. The fight in Mexico had made Hamish look like a monster, what with attacking the referee, and the crowd were not happy with his behaviour.

Los Chicos Valientes got a good cheer. They had once held the Texas Tag Team Titles so they were well known in Dallas. I was worried because Los Chicos had looked the better team in Mexico and Hamish's rage had cost the Scots the match. I so wanted them to win, but Los Chicos were the favourites.

I became even more nervous when dad addressed the crowd with the microphone.

"I'm Bruce Wallace and I'm a Scottish hero," he said before taking a big bite of haggis sausage. "In Scotland, we are real men!"

The crowd booed this for some reason and then Hamish got on the mic.

"But here in Dallas you are not real men," Hamish boomed, getting booed before he even spoke. "That's why they call you cowboys. Not men…boys."

These comments further angered the crowd and they cheered and booed loudly throughout the match.

Most matches in those days started slowly, but this one started with a bang. Poderoso and Elastico hit Hamish with a double dropkick before the bell and dad was furious. He ran over and headbutted Poderoso so hard that we could see the blood dripping out of his nose and through his wrestling mask. The ring mat itself was soon decorated with red spots of blood. It was an explosive start to the title match.

The ref eventually got some control and it was a very even match. The Raging Highlanders made some quick tags at the beginning, but then Dad spent most of the time in the ring and although he took a lot of punishment, he smiled and laughed wildly every time he got hit. This really frustrated the Mexicans and they started trying higher risk moves, most of which they missed. At one point Elastico sprang off the middle rope and hit dad just above the eye with a flying elbow. Suddenly blood was pouring out of dad's head and he just laughed and shouted, "Real men love to bleed!" I was scared for him, but proud at the same time. I had never seen dad like this before.

Dad didn't tag out for over ten minutes. Hamish was screaming at him to tag, but dad just laughed at Hamish. I thought that maybe dad didn't trust Hamish not to enter his newly named Tartan Rage and then lose the match, or maybe dad had lost so much blood that he had really lost his mind.

The match neared its conclusion when Elastico tagged in Poderoso and they hit dad with a vicious double-team move. They first took him down with a double dropkick and then they climbed onto different turnbuckles. Both Mexicans flew through the air and hit dad with a double top-rope leg drop.

1..2..kickout!

Nobody could believe dad had kicked out of that move. The ref told Elastico to leave the ring and Poderoso was standing too near Hamish who punched him from behind. This allowed dad to finally tag Hamish in.

Hamish hammered Poderoso with hard hit after hard hit. Clothesline, slam, suplex, elbow, forearm, powerslam. 1..2..kickout!

Hamish dragged the shattered Poderoso back to his feet getting ready to lift him for the Caber Toss, but Poderoso poked him in the eyes.

RAGE! THE TARTAN RAGE!

Hamish went wild. He slammed Poderoso to the mat hard, then he ran over and clotheslined Elastico off the apron so that he crashed to the floor outside the ring. Still raging, Hamish ran across the ring and bounced off the ropes by dad. As he did this, dad slapped him lightly on the back making a tag. With his eyes burning furiously, Hamish picked up Poderoso and launched him across the ring. Then he picked him up again and Caber Tossed him back to the other side of the ring to where dad was now standing. As Poderoso fell towards dad, his head pointing towards the mat, dad grabbed him by the head in mid-air and smacked him down with a DDT!

1..2..3!

Hamish stared in confusion and dad stood up with blood still covering his face, laughing and smiling.

"The winners," called the ring announcer. "And the first ever World Wrestling Warriors Tag Team Champions of the world… The Raging Highlanders!"

They'd done it! Dad and Hamish were World Champions. I hugged Larry and I even smiled at Firefly. It was amazing! Dad and Hamish were awarded the belts and they held them up to celebrate. The crowd greeted them with more boos, but some people cheered. It was a great match! Hamish and especially my dad Bruce Wallace had looked fantastic. This will always be one of my favourite wrestling matches of all time.

Nightmare Nelmes v Rodeo Joe

The next match helped to calm me down. Rodeo Joe entered first and got a great cheer from his local crowd. Then Nightmare Nelmes came to the ring wearing a black cape, black gloves and a black hat. He looked really weird with the red face paint and vampire teeth flopping around in his mouth. He took the mic and said, "I am Nightmare Nelmes. Fear me. Fear my power. Fear my punches. Fear my hat. I will be your nightmare Rodeo Joe. You will find it hard to sleep after tonight because I am a scary person."

The crowd didn't react to these words at all.

"And I hate cats," Nelmes continued, feeling he had to say more to get the crowd to react to his character like he had been told to by Big Ernie and Hank. "I give cats nightmares. And rabbits. I steal their carrots. I am Nightmare Nelmes. Be scared of me."

The crowd were mostly confused by these comments and some actually laughed. Nobody was scared.

The match was dull, with Nelmes using long submission holds throughout. Rodeo Joe could hardly get a move in and Nelmes finally won when Joe submitted to an armbar. Most of the crowd had gone out to get snacks and drinks. They didn't miss much.

<u>World Wrestling Warriors World Title Match:</u>

<u>Classic Charlie Clean</u>

v

<u>Bruiser Brad Braddock</u>

V

<u>'The Extra-Bert' Bleary O'Leary</u>

The match to be the first ever W.W.W World Champion was the main event and the noise of the crowd was deafening. This was really the fight to be the first ever wrestling champion of the world and therefore it was the biggest wrestling match of all time.

Bleary O'Leary came out first, with his now trademark green suit and hat. He sprinkled Irish Lucky Dust on the crowd and stopped to pour a whole bag onto his son

Larry's head when he reached us, but Larry blew it away and most landed on Firefly.

Bleary got cheered by the crowd who loved his silly antics. When he entered the ring, he lay down on the mat, his hand propping up his head, and whistled while he awaited his opponents.

Bruiser Braddock was next out and he got the biggest boo of the night. I think he got a bit carried away with his character because he actually spat on a fan who shouted in his face as he walked down the entrance ramp. This however, made the crowd boos even louder. When he got into the ring he took the mic and stared at the crowd.

"120,000 people here tonight and I'd just like to tell you…nothing," Bruiser laughed and then dropped the mic. The crowd voiced their anger at him, but he didn't seem to care.

The last to enter was Classic Charlie Clean, the national star and most popular wrestler in the world. His wrestling tights were decorated with the American flag on one leg and the letters C.C.C running down the other. The crowd cheered louder than I had ever heard.

Triple threat matches are fun. The first person to score a pinfall or a submission wins, and you can lose a match even if you are not pinned and you do not submit. The matches are fast and furious and this was one of the best. Bruiser hit Classic, Bleary hit Bruiser, Classic hit Bleary, Bruiser hit Classic. It was intense!

It was like this for about twenty minutes then Bleary O'Leary knocked Bruiser over the top rope with a clothesline. Now the old Bert Doran would have just climbed through the ropes and punched Bruiser, but this was 'The Extra-Bert'. He turned and ran to the opposite side of the ring, bounced off the ropes, ran back across the ring and leapt over the top rope to perform a flying somersault clothesline to Bruiser on the outside. But Bruiser moved and Bleary hit the barriers head first. He was out!

That left Classic and Bruiser to go at it alone. They were well matched. Classic was technically better, but Bruiser was stronger and more aggressive. We had no idea who would win, but like the rest of the crowd we were routing for Classic.

The match's conclusion came when Classic had Bruiser down after hitting him with a spinning elbow. Bruiser looked hurt, but when Classic went to pick him up, Bruiser hit him with a low blow.

'BOO!' the crowd were furious with these cheating tactics, but Bruiser didn't care.

POWERBOMB!

Classic hit the mat hard and this time Bruiser didn't mess about by giving out more punishment. He knew Classic was a great warrior and this was for the World Title. Bruiser went for the cover, but out of the corner of my eye I saw Bleary O'Leary climbing onto a turnbuckle.

1..2..thr.. Bleary O'Leary broke the cover by performing a moonsault off of the turnbuckle and crashing on top of Bruiser's back and neck! The crowd erupted with 'Oohs' and 'Ahhhs'. It was an amazing act of bravery.

Classic was first to his feet and he quickly grabbed Bleary O'Leary who didn't look like he knew where he was. Classic got him into position and hit him with the Clean Sweep.

1..2..3!

"And the first ever W.W.W World Champion...Classic Charlie Clean!"

The crowd were on their feet, joyfully hugging each other and cheering. Classic was given the golden title and he held it aloft. Bleary O'Leary shook his hand and then left him to have his moment of glory alone. A great sportsman and Larry was proud of his dad.

Bruiser was not so sporting however.

"You never beat me did you?" he shouted at Classic, before spitting at him. "You'll never beat me."

Security escorted him from the ring and Classic started to celebrate again. The crowd erupted in cheers once more when Big Ernie Dallas joined Classic in the ring and the two legends celebrated together with the crowd.

We cheered as loud as anyone. It was a great end to a great event. Finally Classic and Big Ernie left the arena and the crowd started to leave. Larry and I then sneaked away and hid in the classroom. Our own Night Of Warriors was about to begin.

Chapter 11: The Beginning

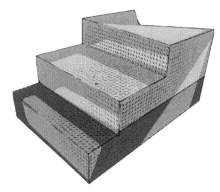

Larry and I waited in that classroom for over an hour, before we were brave enough to come out. It was really strange to find that massive stadium empty after it had been buzzing with noise so recently before.

When we got to the ring, Barry Braddock and Bor were already there. Compared to the wrestlers we had just watched they looked small, but they were a lot bigger than us. But we had been inspired by our dads' performances and by Classic Charlie Clean. This time, I felt we could win.

It might have looked clumsy, but I felt that I was in a classic match. Larry and I used the same tactics as our previous match, dodging and hitting high-flying moves, but we were more aggressive, more confident.

Larry got Bor down with a perfect dropkick.

1..kickout!

I got Bruiser down with a flying clothesline.

1..2..kickout!

But I got caught eventually. I ran across the ring and ducked a punch from Bor, but as I hit the other ropes Barry caught me with a knee in the back. Winded, I ran into Bor and he easily picked me up. POWERSLAM!

1..2..kickout. I still couldn't breathe.

Bor tagged out to Barry and before I could get my breath back I was in the Brad-Lock. Barry was screaming for me to submit, but I wouldn't. This was our Night Of Warriors.

Slowly, I hauled my body over to the ropes. Barry tried to pull me back, but I just managed to get over and tag Larry.

Before Barry could react, Larry hit him with a dropkick. Then a flying clothesline. Then a high knee to the side of the head. Suddenly, Larry jumped onto the turnbuckle and delivered a perfect moonsault onto a standing Barry Braddock, knocking him to the mat.

1..2..thr..kickout.

Both boys struggled back to their feet, Larry the first to react, running off the ropes and trying a high-cross body. But Barry caught him in mid-air and slammed him to the mat. He picked Larry up again and POWERBOMB!

1..2..3!

The match was over, but Barry picked my friend up again. POWERBOMB! I ran into the ring to help, but Bor managed to grab me and powerslammed me to the mat.

Again Braddock picked Larry up and POWERBOMB! I couldn't stop this attack, helplessly held down by Bor.

Braddock picked up Larry for another powerbomb, but a flash of red flew through the air and hit him with a dropkick to the head. Barry Braddock hit the mat and looked up to see a figure standing over him dressed in a red wrestling costume with yellow flames on it, a similar red and yellow cape and an amazing looking red and flaming yellow mask. It was a girl!

She sprang off the ropes and hit Bor with a sliding kick, knocking him off of me.

"Bravo!" a voice called from the crowd. "Bravo!"

It was Big Ernie Dallas, again sitting in the dark of the empty stadium, watching our match. This time he was with the W.W.W trainer Stu Smith. They walked down the steps and into the ring to join us. We were all worried, but Big Ernie had a big smile on his face.

"Well done kids! Well done. You have really impressed me this time, that was actually a good match," Big Ernie said.

"Sorry sir," said Larry.

"Oh I know I told you not to wrestle again, but a determined kid following their dreams is always forgiven. I've been thinking about what to do with you wrestler's kids for a while now. With your dads travelling all over the world with the W.W.W, I wasn't sure what to do with you. You could stay at home with your mums I suppose, or travel with us having school lessons. But you've given me an idea. I'm going to train the stars of tomorrow. I'm going to start the Big Ernie Dallas Wrestling School. Those admitted to it, will travel with the W.W.W having normal school lessons and wrestling lessons with Stu Smith too. It will be way better than normal school. Pupils will get to travel the world and see different cultures. They will leave with a great education. I'll now pay for the best teaching possible. But they'll also get the chance to be a wrestler. To follow their dreams. And you guys, are the first pupils accepted into my school. If that's what you want."

Braddock, Bor, Larry and I all said 'yes' of course. All our dreams had just come true.

"What about girls?" asked the red masked warrior in what was obviously Firefly's voice. "Can we train to wrestle?"

"What do you think Stu?" Big Ernie asked his trainer. "Will you train a girl?"

"After that performance," Stu said smiling at Firefly. "It would be an honour."

Larry and I didn't feel bad about losing the match. Braddock and Bor were bigger and older and we had done ourselves proud. We may have lost, but we were determined to one day beat them. And we were both secretly impressed with Firefly. What a star she had been saving us from those bullies! And we were now in Big Ernie's Wrestling School.

And so, my legendary journey that led to me becoming El Haggisso had truly begun.

The Singles Wrestlers

W.W.W Name:	Real Name:	Origin:	Age:	H: W:	Titles:
Classic Charlie Clean	Charles Clean	New York, USA	37	6:2 235	USA:3 Texas:4 Nevada:3 Canada:2 Mexico:1
Bruiser Brad Braddock	Brad Braddock	London, England	32	6:2 280	UK:3
No-Nonsense Nelmes	Kevin Nelmes	Toronto, Canada	30	6:3 250	Canadian:4
The Extra-Bert Bleary O'Leary	Bert Doran	Ennis, Ireland	30	6:3 250	Irish: 1 UK: 2
Maximum Mike Tullis	Michael Tullis	New Zealand	27	5:7 180	None
Moldaron	Unknown	Unknown	???	6:10 389	None
Caveman Bob	Unknown	Unknown	36	6:9 622	Nigerian: 1 Jamaican:1
Stevie Swing	Steven Barnes	Boston, USA	23	6:0 220	None
El Lobo Negro	Paco Herrero	Mexico City, Mexico	40	5:11 217	Mexican Title:6
Rodeo Joe	Joseph Lambert	Dallas, USA Check	44	6:0 240	Texas:3 Texas Tag: 7 Nevada:2

This is true at the end of this book with the results of the Night Of Warriors event withheld to avoid spoilers.

H = Height   W = Weight (in pounds)

Tag Team Wrestlers

Team:	W.W.W Name:	Real Name:	Origin:	Age:	H: W:	Tag Titles:
The Raging Highlanders (Bax-Stu Boys)	Bruce Wallace	Davie Baxter (Dad)	Edinburgh, Scotland	32	5:9 240	UK:2 Scottish:4
The Raging Highlanders (Bax-Stu Boys)	Hamish MacClan	Mark Stuart	Kirkcaldy, Scotland	28	6:7 320	UK:2 Scottish:4
Los Chicos Valientes	Poderoso	Unknown	Mexico City	32	5:11 213	Mexican: 5 Texas:1
Los Chicos Valientes	Elastico	Unknown	Mexico City	26	6:0 219	Mexican: 5 Texas:1
Russian Bears (Idaho Invincibles)	Igor	David Pike	Boise, Idaho, USA	34	6:0 310	Idaho:5 Canadian: 2 Mexican: 1
Russian Bears (Idaho Invincibles)	Vlad	Jerry Lamb	Boise, Idaho, USA	31	6:3 300	Idaho:5 Canadian: 2 Mexican: 1
Paul + Saul Waters	Paul Waters	Paul Waters	New Jersey, USA	28	5:11 205	New Jersey:3
Paul + Saul Waters	Saul Waters	Saul Waters	New Jersey, USA	29	6:1 218	New Jersey:3

This is true at the end of this book with the results of the Night Of Warriors event withheld to avoid spoilers.

H = Height   W = Weight (in pound)

Your Thoughts On
W.W.W Wrestlers

What did you think about the W.W.W wrestlers?

Write to El Haggisso and tell him which wrestlers you think are the best and why.

Write to him on elhaggisso@gmail.com

Or find him on Twitter and Facebook

Look for El Haggisso books in the future.

This story will continue...

Printed in Great Britain
by Amazon

40947135R00095